Dear Parents:

Congratulations! Your child is taking the first steps on an exciting journey. The destination? Independent reading!

STEP INTO READING® will help your child get there. The program offers five steps to reading success. Each step includes fun stories and colorful art or photographs. In addition to original fiction and books with favorite characters, there are Step into Reading Non-Fiction Readers, Phonics Readers and Boxed Sets, Sticker Readers, and Comic Readers—a complete literacy program with something to interest every child.

Learning to Read, Step by Step!

Ready to Read   Preschool–Kindergarten
• big type and easy words • rhyme and rhythm • picture clues
For children who know the alphabet and are eager to begin reading.

Reading with Help   Preschool–Grade 1
• basic vocabulary • short sentences • simple stories
For children who recognize familiar words and sound out new words with help.

Reading on Your Own   Grades 1–3
• engaging characters • easy-to-follow plots • popular topics
For children who are ready to read on their own.

Reading Paragraphs   Grades 2–3
• challenging vocabulary • short paragraphs • exciting stories
For newly independent readers who read simple sentences with confidence.

Ready for Chapters   Grades 2–4
• chapters • longer paragraphs • full-color art
For children who want to take the plunge into chapter books but still like colorful pictures.

STEP INTO READING® is designed to give every child a successful reading experience. The grade levels are only guides; children will progress through the steps at their own speed, developing confidence in their reading.

Remember, a lifetime love of reading starts with a single step!

Published in the United States by Random House Children's Books, a division of Penguin Random House LLC, 1745 Broadway, New York, NY 10019, and in Canada by Penguin Random House Canada Limited, Toronto.

Step into Reading, Random House, and the Random House colophon are registered trademarks of Penguin Random House LLC.

Visit us on the Web!
StepIntoReading.com
rhcbooks.com

Educators and librarians, for a variety of teaching tools, visit us at RHTeachersLibrarians.com

ISBN 978-0-593-64820-9 (trade) — ISBN 978-0-593-64821-6 (lib. bdg.)

Printed in the United States of America
10 9 8 7 6 5 4 3

Barbie™

YOU CAN BE A TEACHER

adapted by Bria Lymon
based on a story by Gabrielle Reyes
illustrated by Fernando Güell, Ferran
Rodriquez, David Güell, and Jiyoung An

Random House 🏠 New York

Chelsea is excited!
Her sister Malibu
and her friend Brooklyn
will help at her school.

They will learn
what teachers do.

Chelsea shows Malibu and
Brooklyn her classroom.
They meet Ms. Liang.
She is Chelsea's teacher.

Malibu and Brooklyn
meet the class.
Ms. Liang says they
will help her to teach.

The children are building
with blocks.

Malibu helps them.

Now it is time
to clean up.

The children have fun
putting the blocks away.

Ms. Liang gives
Brooklyn wind chimes.
The class knows it is
time to be quiet when
Brooklyn plays them.

The children raise
their hands to show
they are ready to listen.

Everyone sits on
a colorful mat.
Ms. Liang teaches
them a song about
the days of the week.

Brooklyn and Malibu
sing with Ms. Liang.

Ms. Liang shows
Brooklyn all the tools
she uses to teach
in class.

Math time!
Brooklyn helps
Ms. Liang use a video.
It helps her teach
math to the class.

Malibu helps the
children learn to add.

They use buttons
and colorful shapes.

Anthony needs more help.
Malibu has an idea!

She helps him to add
with blocks.
"Good job!"
says Ms. Liang.

It is time to care
for the class pet.
Chelsea brings Miss Nibbleton
some water.
She is thirsty.

Cling! Clang! Boom!

Ms. Laffi teaches
music to the children.

Malibu and Brooklyn
are thrilled at how
the children all join
together to make music!

Brooklyn helps
to teach music.
She strums a guitar.
Ms. Laffi claps along.

Now it is time for lunch!
Brooklyn and Malibu
eat with the children.
They meet the principal.
She is happy they came to help!

It is playtime.

Malibu and Brooklyn

go outside.

They play tag.

Anthony tries to tag Sophie.

26

Brooklyn sees a girl
sitting on a bench.
She and Chelsea
invite her to play.

Time for gym!
Everyone changes
into green shorts
and shirts.

Brooklyn and Malibu
race with the class
around the track.

Time for art!
Malibu and Brooklyn
help Ms. Liang teach the
class to draw a flower.

Ms. Liang says,
"Have fun and do
your best."

Malibu and Brooklyn read a
story to end the school day.
She and Brooklyn have
learned a lot about teaching.
They would be great teachers!

Dear Parents:

Congratulations! Your child is taking the first steps on an exciting journey. The destination? Independent reading!

STEP INTO READING® will help your child get there. The program offers five steps to reading success. Each step includes fun stories and colorful art or photographs. In addition to original fiction and books with favorite characters, there are Step into Reading Non-Fiction Readers, Phonics Readers and Boxed Sets, Sticker Readers, and Comic Readers—a complete literacy program with something to interest every child.

Learning to Read, Step by Step!

Ready to Read   Preschool–Kindergarten
• big type and easy words • rhyme and rhythm • picture clues
For children who know the alphabet and are eager to begin reading.

Reading with Help   Preschool–Grade 1
• basic vocabulary • short sentences • simple stories
For children who recognize familiar words and sound out new words with help.

Reading on Your Own   Grades 1–3
• engaging characters • easy-to-follow plots • popular topics
For children who are ready to read on their own.

Reading Paragraphs   Grades 2–3
• challenging vocabulary • short paragraphs • exciting stories
For newly independent readers who read simple sentences with confidence.

Ready for Chapters   Grades 2–4
• chapters • longer paragraphs • full-color art
For children who want to take the plunge into chapter books but still like colorful pictures.

STEP INTO READING® is designed to give every child a successful reading experience. The grade levels are only guides; children will progress through the steps at their own speed, developing confidence in their reading.

Remember, a lifetime love of reading starts with a single step!

Published in the United States by Random House Children's Books, a division of Penguin Random House LLC, 1745 Broadway, New York, NY 10019, and in Canada by Penguin Random House Canada Limited, Toronto.

Step into Reading, Random House, and the Random House colophon are registered trademarks of Penguin Random House LLC.

Visit us on the Web!
StepIntoReading.com
rhcbooks.com

Educators and librarians, for a variety of teaching tools, visit us at RHTeachersLibrarians.com

ISBN 978-0-593-64820-9 (trade) — ISBN 978-0-593-64821-6 (lib. bdg.)

Printed in the United States of America
10 9 8 7 6 5 4 3

Barbie

YOU CAN BE A FIREFIGHTER

adapted by Bria Lymon
based on a story by Gabrielle Reyes
illustrated by Mattel

Random House 🏠 New York

Malibu and Brooklyn
visit a local fair.
They see a firefighter
at a booth.

They will learn
about firefighters.

5

They meet Fire Chief Elena.
She holds an exit plan.
It shows them where to go
if there is a fire.

"That is a good plan!"
says Brooklyn.

Elena gives Malibu a list
of things firefighters do.
She invites them to the
firehouse to learn more.

Woof!

Brooklyn meets Frankie.

He is the firehouse dog.

Brooklyn cannot wait

to go to the firehouse!

The girls visit the
firehouse the next day.
Elena and Frankie
welcome them.

The other firefighters
are busy at their jobs.
There is a lot to do!

A firefighter shows
them a fire truck.
"Water flows through
this hose," he says.

Malibu wants to help.
She does a nice job
making a tidy rope!

Elena lets Malibu sit
in the fire truck!
"This is fun!" she says.

Next Elena explains
that firefighters
run to keep fit.

Malibu and Brooklyn
start to run.
They want to keep fit, too.
"Good job!" Elena says.

Firefighters must
also be strong.
They jump rope,
lift weights, and cycle.

Malibu and Brooklyn learn that firefighters wear special clothing to keep them safe from fire.

18

Malibu and Brooklyn
try on the
yellow safety pants.

"Firefighters wear bright colors so others can see them through the smoke," says Brooklyn.

The two friends put on
yellow helmets and jackets.
Now they feel like
real firefighters!

Frankie shows them what
to do if they see smoke.

"First we get low!"

says Malibu.

"Then we crawl," says Brooklyn.

23

Malibu and Brooklyn

start to put the gear away.

Ring!

It is the fire alarm!

24

There is a fire!
The firefighters rush
into the fire truck.
The girls will stay away
from danger and follow
Elena's instructions.

The firefighters arrive.

A lady points to the smoke.

"I hope everyone is okay,"

Brooklyn says.

Elena learns the smoke
is coming from a party.
"My grill was on fire,"
a man says.
"But I was able to put it out."

Elena is happy
everyone is safe.
Frankie is happy
to smell the hot dogs.

"Thank you for checking on the fire," the man says. "Remember to always keep a close watch when grilling," says Elena.

Brooklyn and Malibu
go back to the firehouse.
They have learned a lot today.
They would make
great firefighters!